D1264410

ALL THROUGH THE NIGHT

All Through the Night

BY RACHEL FIELD

New York · 1940

THE MACMILLAN COMPANY

FOR

Edith

Lithographed in the United States of America

BY THE DUENEWALD PRINTING CORPORATION

O, what mean these voices singing
All through the night?
O, what mean these bells a-ringing
All through the night?

Old Carol

ALL THROUGH THE NIGHT

All that day the Inn Yard had been thronged with people coming to pay their taxes in the town of Bethlehem. The small sturdy watchdog who slept in the stable and picked up what food he could find had never before seen such a crowd of travelers.

When night fell he was tired from barking at so many strangers and their beasts, and with scurrying out of the way of feet and hoofs. But for all the barking and running about it had been a good day. The Inn had overflowed into the yard. There had been a fire there with meat roasting over it and pots that sent out clouds of savory steam. Many a rich morsel had fallen his way, so he felt well content as he crept into his corner of the stable near the oxen's stall.

He and they greeted each other and exchanged news of the day.

"Yes, we, too, have been busy," the oxen told him. "Heavy loads for us since daybreak and the roads round Bethlehem so choked with carts and caravans and herds and flocks we could hardly move sometimes."

"And rude, stupid creatures they were to meet!" the ass put in from her corner. "With no manners at all or sense enough to follow their own noses. Some even dared to dispute the right of way with me, but I held my ground."

"I have no doubt you did," said the dog, for he knew the ass was not one to be persuaded against her will. He turned himself round and round in a pile of straw to make himself comfortable and fell to licking a bruised spot on his leg.

"There must have been many sheep," the old ewe joined in from her pen. "I could not see them because I was shut in here with my two lambs, but I could tell by their voices that some came from places farther away than Judea. I should have liked to see them."

"Well," the dog told her, "I found them a dusty, frightened lot. I was thankful not to have their herding in my charge. And the goats were no better," he added, that the bearded gray goat

might be sure to hear. He and the goat were not upon friendly terms and took pleasure in tormenting each other.

"Peace and quiet. Peace and quiet at last," the doves cooed from the rafters. "Peace and quiet till morning, that is all we ask."

The hens made soft clucking sounds to show that they were in complete agreement.

But the cock with his scarlet comb and burnished tail feathers, stepping about in search of stray kernels, was of a different mind. "I like noise and bustle myself." He voiced his opinion loudly.

"Peace is all very well for those who haven't the spirit for something better. Now *I* can hardly wait for morning."

"Everyone to his own taste," the mild-eyed cow put in her word, shifting her cud deftly and flicking her tail as she did so. "If it were always day or always night we should not all be satisfied."

"Well said. Well said," the doves agreed in drowsy unison from the dimness of the eaves.

Darkness gathered there first. The swallows were already seeking their nests, while the bats were beginning to stretch and unfold their lean, black wings.

Night was coming fast and all the birds and beasts and insects of the stable knew that it belonged to them. The world was theirs as the world of day could never be. When the sun rose man would be their master again. They would carry his burdens or feed or serve him according to their different gifts. But night was their own, when they might move or fight or take counsel together without man's interference. It was good that this should be so, the little dog thought, as he burrowed deeper into the straw.

His sworn enemy the cat slid by. She moved like a shadow with fiery-green eyes ready to pounce upon the mice who were already squeaking and scampering at their play. But the dog was too tired and comfortable to give chase, so for once he let her pass unmolested. All about him crickets chirped in rusty chorus and sometimes a bat swooped so low he could feel the stir of its wings. The darkness was warm and alive with the familiar scents of fur and feathers and grain and straw.

"Rest well. Rest well. Rest well." The doves cooed sleepily, making a soft

sound in their throats that was like the
bubbling of a well-filled pot over a fire.

Night had come to Bethlehem. The
Inn had been full hours ago. The dog
could hear late travelers being turned
away. The stable door was securely
bolted against intruders and the wind
was rising, frosty and keen. Through an
opening in the roof a star shone bright
as purest silver.

"I never saw a star look so large or so near," the cock observed as he moved about with his spurred, high-stepping walk. "Somehow it makes me very restless, and there is something strange in the air. Perhaps you have felt it, too?"

But the dog made no answer. He yawned and laid his pointed muzzle on his paws and prepared himself for sleep.

He woke at the sound of voices out-
side and roused himself to bark. But
though the hair rose along his back, no
sound came rumbling from his throat.
The bolt was drawn and the stable door
opened to lantern light and the dim
shapes of two men and a donkey on
whose back a woman sat, wrapped in a
heavy cloak.

"Well"—the voice of the Inn Keeper sounded short and impatient—"if you cannot go on, there is only the stable to offer. Coming as you have at such an hour, you are fortunate to have this shelter till morning."

"The roads were crowded," the Man answered him, "and our pace was slow because of my wife. You can see that she is nearly spent."

"Yes, yes." The Inn Keeper was already shutting the door. "I am sorry for your plight, but I tell you there is no room left."

The dog was on his feet. He could hear the other animals rising about him, yet not one of them uttered a sound. Their throats were as silent as his own.

In the flickering lantern light he watched the Man lift the Woman from the donkey's back and set her upon her feet. She was so weary she would have fallen but for the Man's arms.

"Joseph," she said, "you must not be troubled for me, even if it should be that the time has come." . . . She rested her head on the Man's shoulder and sighed so softly it might have been one of the doves in the rafters drawing closer to her mate.

"But, Mary," the Man went on, "it is not right and fitting that it should be here,—not in a stable among the beasts."

"Who knows," she comforted him, "what is to be? These beasts are more kind than men who kill and hurt one another. I am glad to be here. Their warm breath comforts me. Their straw is clean and soft to rest upon."

Everywhere beyond the ring of light that the lantern made, bright eyes were upon the strangers. Furry ears and quivering noses pointed, alert and watchful.

The strange donkey, freed of his load, found a place beside the ass. He sank down, too tired to drink water from the trough or reach for a mouthful of hay.

A hush was on the stable. Not only were all throats silent, but no wings stirred; no claws scratched and not a hoof pounded. And in that hour nothing died. The young swallows and mice were safe from their enemies, for a mystery greater than death held them all in its power.

The lantern flickered and went out.

"Our oil is gone!" the Man cried out in distress.

"There will be light enough." The Woman spoke in a faint voice, and as if in answer the star in the roof gap shone brighter than before.

How long it was after that the little dog could not tell. Morning was still far off, yet the cock suddenly lifted up his voice, so shrill and clear it seemed he would split himself in two. It was not like any other cockcrow since the world began and it rose higher than the rafters and mounted to heaven itself. At the same instant each creature found voice and joined with him. Every living thing in the stable had a part in that swelling chorus of praise. Even the bees hummed till their hive throbbed with music, sweeter than all its store of honey.

"What manner of place is this?" the Man cried out. "What beasts are these who have the tongues of angels?"

But the Woman answered him softly out of the shadows. "It was they who gave us shelter this night. Let them draw near and be the first to worship."

She drew aside the folds of her cloak and light filled the stable even to the farthest corners. The dog cowered before such strange brightness. When he dared to look more closely he saw that it encircled the head of an infant, new born.

"There is no bed for him to lie upon," the Man sighed. "Only this"—and he pointed to the manger.

"Bring it here," the Mother said. "My heart tells me there will be nights when he will have no place at all to rest his head."

So the Child lay quiet in the straw-filled wooden manger and all the animals came to view him there—the oxen, the cow, the ass and the donkey, the ewe and her lambs, the gray goat, the dog, the hens and the proud cock ruffling his feathers. The cat left off her prowling to join them and the mice ran beside her without fear. The crickets came, too, drawn from the comfort of their warm straw; the bees, from their snug hive. The tireless ants and spiders left their toil to draw near. The swallows in the eaves flew down; the bats bent low on their dark wings, and the doves came closest of all with their soft murmurs above the manger. When they had all seen the Wonder they returned to their places and were quiet again.

All but the dog. He could not rest as he had before. He stretched himself beside the manger and lay with his head

on his folded paws, his eyes wide and watchful as the hours passed.

Long before sunrise the door opened without sound of bolt being drawn and a band of Shepherds came in. They bore a strange tale on their lips and they also worshiped on bended knees. One carried a lamb in his arms and the Child answered its bleating with a smile.

"Behold the Lamb of God," they said one to another as they turned to go back to their flocks on the hills.

The star grew pale and through the gap in the stable roof morning showed rosy in the east. Even before the cock hailed it, the dog knew that the sun was up. But he did not move lest he rouse the three in his care. It was then that he saw a strange thing.

The rafters high above cast their shadows as the rising sun struck through. Two of the beams crossed in sharp black bars that fell directly across the sleeping Child. The little dog could not tell why the sight should make him cower in sudden fear.

Then the cock crowed three times and the first sounds of people stirring in the Inn and yard began.

He watched the Man and the Woman preparing to go. He saw the donkey being watered and fed and the blanket fitted in place. He saw the Mother wrap her Son warmly against the cold before the Man set them upon the donkey's back and lifted a heavy bundle on his own.

"Come," he said and opened the stable door. "We must make haste."

Stiff from his long vigil, the dog rose and followed them to the door. He watched them cross the Inn yard in the early light and join other travelers who were already thronging the roads leading to and from Bethlehem. Soon they would be lost to his sight, those Three whom he had guarded through the hours of darkness.

"Ah," cried the cock, preening his burnished feathers, "what a morning!" He strutted over to where bits of food and grain lay scattered and began to forage for stray morsels.

The dog lifted his head and sniffed hungrily. He could tell that pots were already on the fires. The sharp morning air brought the savory news to him and he knew that by keeping close to the kitchen he would soon be well filled. He remembered a bone he had buried yesterday in a secluded spot. Yet he did not seek it. He trotted past the kitchen doors, and though his nose twitched at the smells that he was leaving he kept it pointed straight ahead.

"Wait. Wait." His bark rang out sharp and determined and his paws clicked over the stones as he ran.

He did not pause till he had caught up with the Man who led the plodding donkey and his burden along the dusty road.

"Here I am!" He barked again as he fell into step beside them. "Let me come with you."